◆MARC BROWN◆

WHAT DO YOU CALL A DUMB BUNNY?

AND OTHER RABBIT RIDDLES, GAMES, JOKES, AND CARTOONS

COPYRIGHT © 1983 BY MARC BROWN

Library of Congress Cataloging in Publication Data

Brown, Marc Tolon.
What do you call a dumb bunny?

Summary: A collection of rabbit humor and puzzles, including some illustrated facts about rabbits.
1. Rabbits – Anecdotes, facetiae, satire, etc.
2. Wit and humor, Juvenile [1. Rabbits – Wit and humor.
2. Rabbits – Miscellanea] I. Title.
PN6231.R23B7 1983   818'.5402   82-21650
ISBN 0-316-11117-1
ISBN 0-316-11119-8 (pbk.)
HC: 10 9 8 7 6 5 4
PB: 10 9 8 7 6 5

JOY STREET BOOKS ARE PUBLISHED BY LITTLE, BROWN AND COMPANY (INC.)

BP

Published simultaneously in Canada by Little, Brown & Company (Canada) Limited
PRINTED IN THE UNITED STATES OF AMERICA

WHAT HAS TWO FUZZY PINK EARS AND WRITES?

I'VE ALREADY HEARD THAT ONE, A BALLPOINT BUNNY.

PLUS A RACE BETWEEN A HARE AND A TORTOISE.

AND TWO FLIP BOOKS, ONE IS A HAIR RAISING EXPERIENCE!

CONTENTS

WHAT'S THE BEST WAY TO CATCH A TAME RABBIT?

THE "TAME" WAY

HOW MANY HAIRS IN A RABBIT'S TAIL?

NONE, THEY ARE ALL ON THE OUTSIDE

HOW ARE RABBITS LIKE CALCULATORS?

WHY CAN'T A RABBIT'S NOSE BE TWELVE INCHES LONG?

FAMOUS RABBITS

RABBITSON CRUSOE

LEONARDO DA VABBIT

RABBITSTEIN'S MONSTER

THOMAS ALVA RABBITSON

RUDOLPH THE RED NOSED RABBIT

RABBIT HOOD

PROFESSOR HAREBRAIN'S RABBIT QUIZ

TRUE
OR
FALSE

1. SOME RABBITS CAN JUMP 15 FEET.

2. RABBITS' TEETH GROW 4 INCHES EACH YEAR - THAT'S WHY THEY NIBBLE SO MUCH.

3. WHAT IS A RABBIT'S FAVORITE MOVIE MUSICAL?

4. MOST RABBITS LIVE 5 OR 6 YEARS BUT SOME LIVE 13 YEARS.

5. RABBITS HAVE BEEN KNOWN TO HIDE IN TREES.

6. RABBITS LIVE IN SWAMPS, MARSHES, DESERTS, AND FORESTS.

7. RABBITS WITH WHITE FUR AND PINK EYES ARE CALLED ALBINOS.

8. FOR 2000 YEARS PEOPLE HAVE TAMED RABBITS FOR PETS.

9. MOST RABBITS SHED THEIR COATS THREE OR FOUR TIMES A YEAR.

10. A RABBIT'S FAVORITE FEEDING TIME IN THE WILD IS DAWN OR DUSK.

(ANSWERS: 1,2,4,5,6,7,8,9,10 ALL TRUE. 3, HARE)

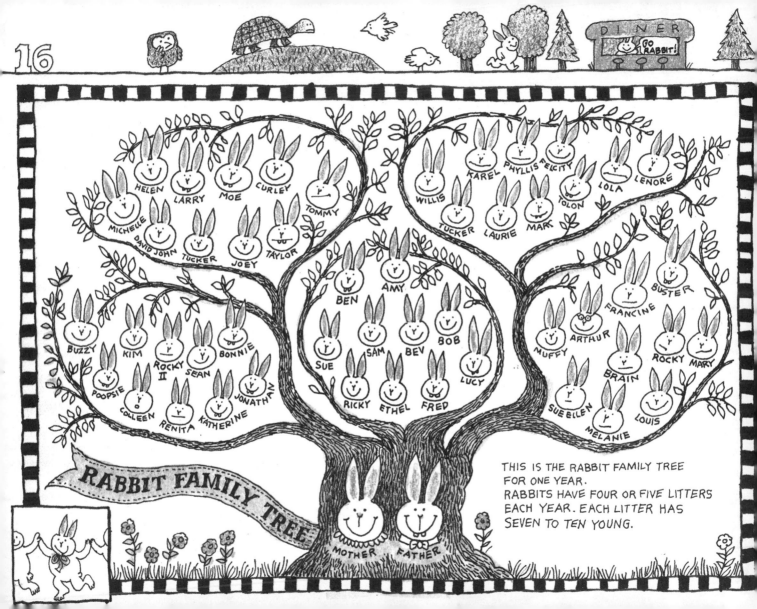

THIS IS THE RABBIT FAMILY TREE
FOR ONE YEAR.
RABBITS HAVE FOUR OR FIVE LITTERS
EACH YEAR. EACH LITTER HAS
SEVEN TO TEN YOUNG.

RABBIT FAMILY TREE

THE EASTER BUNNY

THE FIRST EASTER BUNNY MAY HAVE LOOKED SOMETHING LIKE THIS. THE IDEA OF THE EASTER BUNNY IS VERY OLD. IT BEGAN IN ANCIENT EGYPT WHERE THE HARE WAS THE SYMBOL OF THE MOON. THE DATE OF EASTER DEPENDS ON THE MOON.

2 WAYS TO HOLD A RABBIT

NEVER PICK UP A RABBIT BY THE EARS.

HARES AND RABBITS ARE DIFFERENT

HARE	RABBIT
○ LARGE SIZE	○ SMALL SIZE
○ LONG EARS	○ SHORT EARS
○ FAST RUNNER	○ NOT A DISTANCE RUNNER
○ COLOR CHANGES WITH THE SEASON	○ COLOR STAYS THE SAME
○ ARE BORN WITH FUR	○ NOT BORN WITH FUR
○ CAN SEE AT BIRTH	○ BORN BLIND
○ CAN RUN SHORTLY AFTER BIRTH	○ BORN TOO WEAK TO RUN

MUNCHY MAZE

BOTH HARES AND RABBITS ARE VEGETARIANS. GO THROUGH THE MAZE AND DISCOVER WHAT THEY LIKE TO EAT.

LEAVES • CLOVER • ALFALFA • LETTUCE • CARROTS • OATS • DANDELIONS • CABBAGE • HAY • GARDEN PLANTS • KALE • BRAN • BOILED POTATOES • GRASS

YUM YUM

WHAT KIND OF RABBITS LIVE AT THE NORTH POLE?

WHAT DO RABBITS HAVE THAT NOTHING ELSE HAS?

WHAT IS A RABBIT'S FAVORITE DANCE?

THE BUNNY HOP

Panel 1

WHY CAN A RABBIT HOP HIGHER THAN THE EMPIRE STATE BUILDING?

THE EMPIRE STATE BUILDING CAN'T HOP.

Panel 2

HOW CAN YOU TELL A RABBIT FROM A GORILLA?

A RABBIT DOESN'T LOOK LIKE A GORILLA.

WHAT KINDS OF RABBITS EAT WITH THEIR EARS?

ALL RABBITS EAT WITH THEIR EARS. THEY CAN'T TAKE THEM OFF.

WHAT KIND OF BOOK DOES A RABBIT LIKE AT BEDTIME?

ONE WITH A HOPPY ENDING.

THREE LITTLE BUNNIES

1 HEAD

2 EARS

3 EYES AND NOSE

4 MOUTH AND TEETH

5 FRONT LEGS

6 HIND LEGS

7 PUFFY TAIL

8 BLACK TIE

DINER

DRAW YOUR OWN RABBIT

RABBIT TONGUE TWISTERS

SAY EACH TONGUE TWISTER THREE TIMES, AS FAST AS YOU CAN.

BENNY BUNNY BOUGHT A BETTER BIKE THAN BETTY BUNNY.

BABY BUNNIES RIDE IN BABY BUGGIES.

BILLY'S BIG BAD BUNNY BLEW BUBBLES.

WHAT A DUMB BUNNY!

DINER

CLOSE ENCOUNTERS
OF THE FUZZY KIND

U.F.B.
UNIDENTIFIED
FLYING BUNNY

BUNNY'S
TRUCK STOP
EAT HERE
GET GAS

CRUNCHY CARROT INC.

CAN WE GET SOME GAS?

LOOK!

WAITRESS, WHAT'S THIS HARE DOING IN MY SOUP?

I DIDN'T SEE IT.

LOOKS LIKE THE BACKSTROKE.

LET ME OUT, THIS PLACE IS GROSS.

WHAT A DUMP.

OH SURE, JUST EAT THE CHILI.

BURP.

GAS PETROL

GAS PETROL

PLAY THE PIANO

THE SECRET LIFE OF RABBITS
THINGS YOU NEVER SEE RABBITS DO

FLY A KITE

PLAY DRESS-UP

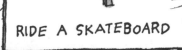

RIDE A SKATEBOARD

RIDE A TRICYCLE

HOW TO MAKE A RABBIT SHADOW

GET SOME OF YOUR FRIENDS TOGETHER AND MAKE SOME RABBIT SHADOWS OR HAVE A RABBIT SHADOW PLAY. SEE HOW MANY OTHER SHADOW ANIMALS YOU CAN MAKE WITH YOUR HANDS.

RIDICULOUS RABBIT DISGUISES

HUMAN NOSE

WILD GLASSES

MOUSTACHE

FANGS

HUMAN EARS

BEARD

MONSTER RABBIT

BAD BUNNY

GOOD GUY

REGULAR RABBIT

TAB

TAB

ASTRO BUNNY

WITCH RABBIT

MAKE YOUR OWN FINGER PUPPETS
TRACE AND COLOR, THEN CUT OUT AND TAPE TABS TOGETHER.
MAKE UP SOME OF YOUR OWN CHARACTERS AND STORIES. HAVE FUN!